BE A STAR!

BY MALIQUE WASHINGTON

For someone I could never repay—
My beloved grandfather, James "The invincible" Kelson

Acknowledgements: I am forever grateful for Ms. Love, the school librarian, who guided me throughout the process of creating this story. Your support and guidance was simply amazing. Special thanks to my friends, teammates, educators, coaches, and all who impacted my life. Huge thanks to my parents, siblings, cousins, aunts, uncles, and grandparents for being my greatest supporters. Finally, I want to thank all young readers, for you inspire me more than you could ever imagine. The world is yours. Thank you, from the bottom of my heart.

Malique's class was reaching
the end of the day.

"Papa had amazing cooking skills.
He loved to cook mouthwatering foods
for the family.

Papa would make spaghetti, barbeque,
tamales, and tacos.

And fried chicken, candy yams,
taquitos, and nachos!"

"With belief, Papa was able
to play football at a college where
it was cold and chill.
He did amazing things, and
had an awesome thrill."

am Team, Jim Kelson

James Kelson was voted into the University of Northern Colorado's 50 Year Football Dream Team in the 2000's as a linebacker.

"College was definitely not a breeze.
But my amazing Papa worked hard, and got two degrees!"

“As a teacher and principal, my Papa influenced many people like me and you.

If you want to become a star, you must believe in yourself because that’s what stars do.”

Amazing was Mr. K., I'm becoming a fan.
If you believe you can do something, you certainly can!"

Mr. Booker said as he smiled and stood up from his desk.

" My Papa was a family man first.

He believed in being kind to loved ones...

Even at your worst! "

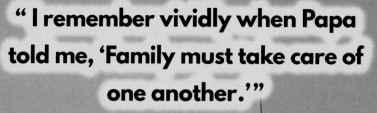

" I remember vividly when Papa told me, 'Family must take care of one another.'"

"Always be kind to your siblings and parents, but especially your mother."

ABOUT MR. BOOKER

Devin Booker's inspirational rise to the top of the basketball world inspired the author to honor him as the class teacher in BE A STAR! Devin Booker is perhaps best known for his legendary 70 point performance against the Boston Celtics on March 24, 2017. He became the youngest player ever to score 60 points, and only the 6th player in NBA history to score 70. Devin was also the 2018 NBA 3 Point Shootout Champion, and went on to break the records for the most points in a single round, and the most points in the final round. In March of 2019, at 22 years of age, Devin Booker became the youngest player of all-time with consecutive 50 point games. This past season, Devin received his first, but long overdue NBA all star selection at the age of 23.

Most importantly, Devin is just an awesome guy. He's a philanthropist, 2k master, a leader in his community, highly intelligent, and wise beyond his years. Follow the young star on Instagram & Facebook– @dbook, and Twitter @devinbook. He is truly a star in his own, unique way, and so are you!

ABOUT THE AUTHOR

Malique Washington has won numerous awards and accolades for the success of BE A STAR!. Growing up with a vicious stuttering disability was very hard for Malique, but this only made him stronger, and inspired him to win in life. From the principles you learned in BE A STAR!, taught by the author and his beloved grandfather, Malique Washington was able to become a standout student-athlete, author, lifelong learner, and inspirational speaker. He is a living example that there is a star in every kid, no matter their circumstance or adversity. Malique's journey is only beginning, and he wants to continue to inspire young stars like you around the globe to think big, and become the person that they were born to be. You are a star!

#BeaStar

Follow Malique on Facebook, Instagram, and Twitter-- @maliquewash